KIDS CAN PRESS

SALESMAN OF THE MONTH

I can sell anything!
See for yourself...

We could go on and on.

But I know what you're thinking: "AL, I don't need all this incredible stuff. I just need a GREAT BOOK!"

Storybooks that put you to sleep!

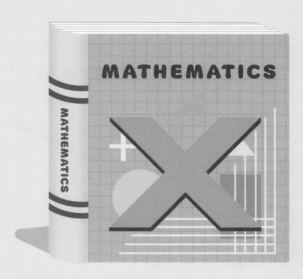

Schoolbooks that add up to ZERO fun!

Cookbooks that leave a bad taste in your mouth!

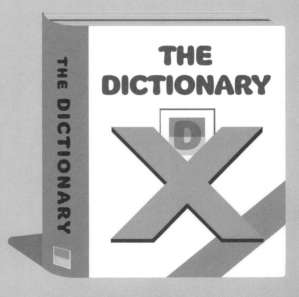

And the dictionary — a book so boring even words can't describe it!

Let me take a moment
to compliment you.

The outfit you're wearing is simply breathtaking! It really brings out the color of your eyes!

Now, my friend, let's talk business.

I LIKE YOU.
So, I'll make you
an offer you
can't refuse!

If you buy my book in the next 10 seconds, I will throw in your very own, top-of-the-line ...

Not convinced?

Research shows that **100% of my customers** noticed a dramatic increase in happiness after buying my book.

BEFORE AFTER

Have I got a book for you!

AMAZING transformation!!!

the ending is really gr8
end

This small print is here to inform you that the frog above is a paid professional actor. Results and smiles may vary.

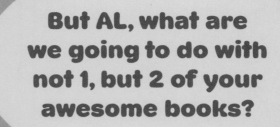

gift for a loved one

unique hat

**hassle-free
door stopper**

decorative coaster

mat that will make
you look inches taller

The possibilities
are endless,
my friend!!!

or really cool thing
to hide behind

Now, just
imagine what
you can do with

**742
books!**

YES,

it's the

Book Fort

you've

always

wanted!

duct tape not included

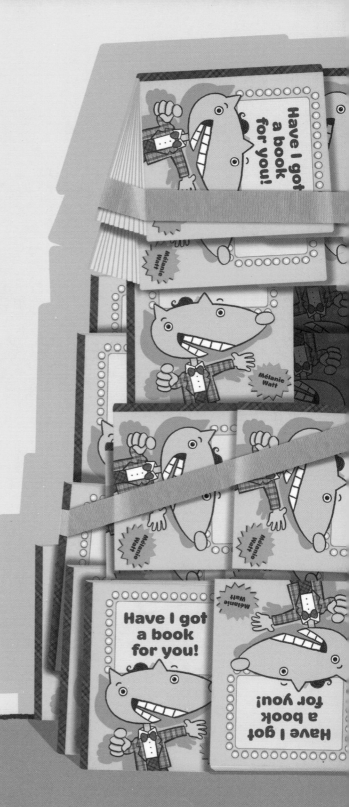

I'm warning you, my books are in high demand!

They're flying off the shelves!

Buy now! Quantities are limited ...

DEDICATION

For my friend Tara, who truly deserves the EDITOR OF THE MONTH plaque for buying into all my ideas, especially this cheesy one.

Kids Can Press acknowledges the financial support of the Government of Ontario, through the Ontario Media Development Corporations Ontario Book Initiative; the Ontario Arts Council; the Canada Council for the Arts; and the Government of Canada, through the BPIDP, for our publishing activity.

Published in Canada by
Kids Can Press Ltd.
29 Birch Avenue
Toronto, ON M4V 1E2

Published in the U.S. by
Kids Can Press Ltd.
2250 Military Road
Tonawanda, NY 14150

www.kidscanpress.com

The artwork in this book was rendered in charcoal pencil and assembled digitally.
The text is set in Hamburger Font BF.

Edited by Tara Walker
Designed by Mélanie Watt
Printed and bound in China

This book is smyth sewn casebound.

CM 09 0 9 8 7 6 5 4 3 2

LIBRARY AND ARCHIVES CANADA CATALOGUING IN PUBLICATION

Watt, Mélanie, 1975–

   Have I got a book for you! / written and illustrated by Mélanie Watt.

ISBN 978-1-55453-289-6 (bound)

I. Title.

PS8645.A884H38 2009   C813'.6   2008-908122-6

Kids Can Press is a l̑ȎȓȖS™ Entertainment company